Sow the Wind

STEPHANIE A. CAIN

BOOKS BY STEPHANIE A. CAIN

STORMS IN AMETHIR
Stormsinger
Stormshadow
Stormseer
The Weather War
Witchery's End (forthcoming)

FAITH AND FEALTY
Sow the Wind

CIRCLE CITY MAGIC
Shades of Circle City
Circle City Psychic
"C" in *E is for Evil* (ed. Rhonda Parrish)
"G" in *F is for Fairy* (forthcoming – ed. Rhonda Parrish)

WITH OTHERS
Equus (ed. Rhonda Parrish)

This is a work of fiction. Names, characters, places, and incidents are the product of the author's imagination. Any resemblance to actual persons, living or dead, is entirely coincidental.

ISBN: 978-0-9903758-2-1
First Paperback Printing, August 2014
Published by Cathartes Press

DEDICATION

This one is for Jillian Storm,
because she asked me to write it.

ACKNOWLEDGMENTS

Thanks are due to more people than I can mention, but here are a few: Cathy and Steve Daniel, who introduced my parents to Middle-earth before I was born, and their amazing family: Mandy, Preston and Dacia, Kyle and Anna, Neil and Elyse. Laura VanArendonk Baugh, always. Jillian Storm, who I sometimes believe loves Justin even more than I do. Jack King, who has been an encourager since we met two years ago. Jessica Miller, who suffered through some of my earliest attempts at writing. My favorite independent bookstore, Robots and Rogues in Lafayette, Indiana.

I am also grateful to the talented Phuoc Quan, who possesses a magical ability to take my fumbling descriptions and reference images and turn them into a beautiful cover that perfectly represents my story.

CHAPTER ONE

Gabriel Malnythe braced himself against a stone merlon and strained to see any disturbance of the tall march grass. The gentle swell of the land north of Jerol was empty of activity, save the flurry of grouse wings. Behind him, workers in the courtyard carried food from the storehouse to the kitchens. The blacksmith labored over his forge; the steady ring of the hammer mocked the way Gabriel's heart kept stuttering and leaping.

Footsteps approached on the stone rampart and someone chuckled. "I've never seen you wait with such ill grace."

Gabriel turned, his lips curling ruefully. "They should have been here yesterday. Forgive me for being worried about my cousin. Too many things could happen to the prince on his way here."

Sir Jon Carter was a big man. He grinned down at Gabriel, the breeze ruffling his dark hair. "And the fact this is Ran's first visit back home in two years has nothing to do with it." Ranulf Destry, Gabriel's dearest friend, had been gone to the Elite Corps for two years, ever since Gabriel had put off his own decision about joining the group of human weapons who guarded the royal family.

Gabriel rubbed his jaw and looked out over the marches. "Laurenstat changes a lot of men." It had certainly changed him.

"That's uncharitable of you, my lord. If you think the capital could change *him*--"

"No." Gabriel sighed. "You're right, of course. I allow my own self-doubt to make me doubt him. Ranulf has never been anything but kind, honorable, and loyal. You're right to rebuke me."

Jon just grunted in response.

Gabriel decided to let the subject go. "Is everything ready for the prince's arrival?"

"As much as I can control, it is. Sergeant Savona has rotations drawn up for extra guards. The household staff has prepared the suite next to yours for Prince Justin's use. Quarters are ready for the Elite Corps. I need your signature on some of the requisitions I made." Jon held out a sheaf of papers and a pen.

Gabriel only scanned each page before scrawling his name across the bottom. He enjoyed the way running his father's estate demanded diplomacy and thinking creatively to solve problems; he was not so keen on the administrative paperwork. "I am grateful Uncle Godfric places so much trust in us," he said as he signed the last, "but I confess, my mind is easier when we are visiting Justin at the palace."

"I promise your mind is still easier than Captain Hakin's or Sergeant Savona's. Savona actually snapped at me when I asked about the prince's accommodations."

Gabriel smirked. "Because you'd probably already asked her twice."

"There are times," Jon said, "when the fact you're my liege lord is all keeps me from smacking you."

"There." Gabriel lifted a slender hand to point at standards on the horizon. "I see the prince's device." He grinned at Jon and ran down the steps to the courtyard, where his horse was saddled and waiting.

They met the prince's party half a mile from the keep. The dark-haired prince dismounted at the same time Gabriel did. The cousins embraced, Justin letting go a moment before Gabriel.

"Saints, you've grown," Gabriel blurted. "You're a good handbreadth taller than the last time I saw you."

Justin slapped his cousin on the shoulder. "Wait til you see my muscles," he boasted. Gabriel fought a grin. His cousin was often solemn for his age, but sometimes it was obvious he was only fourteen.

"I heard you've gone to mastery level in your sword--" Gabriel cut himself off as Baronet Brandon Shrike, the Prince's Knight, approached. A stark figure in his black uniform, Shrike spared neither smile nor greeting for Gabriel.

"Duchess Elna approaches," he told Justin. "Try to act like a prince when greeting her son."

Gabriel bit his tongue to keep from pointing out that princes could greet their cousins however they chose. His mother had traveled with the prince's contingent from the capital, and she would expect the guestright ceremony. Ranulf, riding alongside the duchess' carriage, grinned at Gabriel and tilted his head ever so slightly. Damn propriety, anyway; Gabriel longed to greet Ranulf openly despite matters of rank. Instead he bowed to the prince.

"Cousin, welcome. You honor us with your visit."

Justin's mutinous expression faded. "I--ah, you honor me by hosting us." He glanced around. "Do you hold by the guestright, cousin?"

In answer, Gabriel held out a water flask. "Wash the dust of travel from your hands and heart, honored guests." When Justin extended his hands, palm up, Gabriel poured the water over them. He did the same for the Prince's Knight, Jon, and Ranulf, then rinsed his own hands. Next he took a flask of wine and offered a sip to each of them in the same order as before, pouring the remainder of the flask out as an offering to the Gods.

"As we have shared water and wine, you are my guest," Gabriel said. "May the Just Goddess smite me and the Merciful God turn from me if I do not also shed my blood for you, should it be needed."

Justin and Gabriel clasped hands and the ritual was complete. Gabriel had welcomed the prince's party and extended his protection to the prince and all those with him.

"No doubt you are worn from travel," Gabriel said. "Come, I have a feast prepared for you."

As they headed back towards the keep, he rode alongside the prince, who chattered about the vast openness of the plains and how good it was to get out of the capital. Occasionally Justin threw remarks over his shoulder at Brandon Shrike, though Shrike largely ignored them in favor of exchanging news with Jon. Gabriel tried to stay focused on the prince, but something Brandon Shrike said caught his attention.

"How are things in Laurenstat?" Jon had asked.

Shrike grunted. "Political. The council wants Godfric to put Ariana aside and take a young queen to bear more children. The clerics disagree, both with the council and with each other. Thank the Saints Godfric gave me an excuse to get Justin away from all that."

"Because it's such a hardship for you to accompany the prince on holiday," Jon teased.

"It wouldn't be if the little brat knew how to do as he's told," Brandon muttered.

The conversation had caught Justin's attention too. "The little brat can hear you," he called back.

"Bratling princes who eavesdrop deserve everything that's said about them," Brandon retorted. Justin fought a grin and ducked his head. Gabriel smiled. It was good to see his cousin happy. When he looked out across the plains again, he straightened in the saddle.

"Justin, look. There are others who wish to pay their respects." A score of riders were approaching at an angle to intercept them before they reached the keep.

Justin followed his gaze. "Are they Shallans? I've never met any Shallans before. Father said I should take advantage of this trip to learn their customs."

"Those are Sweetgrass Clan," Gabriel said. "See the red horses? And the warriors all wear the same golden ribbons in their hair that they braid into the horses' tails."

Shrike urged his horse closer and gripped Gabriel's elbow. "These Sweetgrass. Are they safe?"

Gabriel lifted his chin. "They swore the water treaties with my father's grandsire. Two score of them defended my life when the Bitterfruit Uprising caught us out on the Free Marches. Justin is safer than he would be at the Laurenstat docks."

Justin cleared his throat. "How shall I greet them, Gabriel? Do they speak our tongue?"

"Call them Sweetgrass Herd of the Horse Clans," he advised. "Shallan is our name for them, not theirs. Say *dothai hal* first. It's a wish for the Gods' blessing on the person you greet. Then greet them as you would any other lord. You see the one with the painted shield and the lance with all the ribbons? That's the chieftain, River Thunder. He's doing you courtesy to come greet you."

"The Sweetgrass Clan have made blood treaties with us," Justin began, but Gabriel cut him off with a gesture.

"Water treaties," he corrected. "The Horse Clans swear blood treaties only in war. Those treaties are good, but water are better."

Justin's shoulders slumped. "I'll never remember. Water doesn't seem better."

Gabriel hummed. "Here's how I learned to keep them straight. In war, your ally agrees to help you shed blood. But in any circumstance, your true friend gives you water to drink."

Behind them, Shrike snorted. "Makes no sense. Blood's more worth than water."

"Has it?" Gabriel arched an eyebrow at him. "You can't grow crops or nourish horses on blood. Blood is only valuable to the person who loses it. Water does good to those who receive it."

"Spoken like a man who's afraid of a good fight," Shrike muttered.

Gabriel saw Justin frown, but he didn't want to argue. He tightened his legs around his horse to urge him forward.

5

"Come along, Justin. I'm eager to introduce you to my friends."

The welcoming feast was a merry event. Jerol's holders and tenants gathered in the banquet hall and rubbed elbows with Elite Corps, nobles, and Shallans. No, Justin reminded himself. Horse Clans. Learn who they truly are, so you can learn how to love them. He cast a longing look at the serving girl who carried the bottle of Sweetgrass mead.

"Some lass catch your eye?" Brandon's voice was close in Justin's ear, making the prince shiver.

"Not some lass," he replied. "Some grass. Sweetgrass."

"One cup is enough for a skinny brat like you," Brandon said. "You can't get drunk at the welcome feast. Save some of your fun for later."

Justin huffed a sigh. "As if you would let me do *anything* fun while we're here. Saints witness, you're worse than my old nursemaid."

He knew why Brandon was being so cautious. King Godfric hadn't wanted to let Justin leave Laurenstat. He'd had scores of reasons against it, but Justin had worn his father down. His father refused to see Justin was on the doorstep of manhood, but Justin was determined to make him see. After all, he was training to be a swordmaster, and some of the boys he'd grown up with were squiring for lords who could teach them diplomacy and land management as well as the arts martial.

Brandon's superior in the Elite Corps had insisted on a strong protective detail to accompany the prince. Justin's father didn't like Brandon, but he had voiced no objection to putting Brandon in command of the excursion. The only conclusion Justin could draw from that was his father planned to rid himself of Justin's best friend if anything happened on this visit.

"And you're acting like a spoiled child instead of a supposedly responsible prince," Brandon growled.

Justin shrugged away from the hand on his shoulder. The feast hall was stuffy and ablaze with light, but it felt friendly, happy. Justin wanted to enjoy it. If Brandon hadn't grown so gloomy over the past few months... But he pushed aside those thoughts.

"Justin--" Brandon began, but Justin turned a fierce look on him and he fell silent.

"My father told you to protect me." Justin kept his voice low and attempted to warm his expression. He mustn't appear displeased or ungrateful, lest it insult Gabriel's people. "He did not tell you to cut my meat and chew it for me."

The words were churlish. He knew even before Brandon's cheeks flushed. But Justin would not recall them. He unbent his pride enough to say, "You've looked forward to seeing that friend of yours. Jon? Go spend some time with him. I am safe."

Brandon held Justin's gaze for so long Justin almost feared he would disobey. Then he saluted and spun on his heel. Justin almost pitied this Jon Carter. Then again, anyone who befriended the prickly nobleman would surely know what he was in for.

Justin looked from his protector's retreating back to the serving girl with the mead. He gestured her over to refill his cup, then went in search of his cousin.

Gabriel was slouched at the head of the table, a lazy smile on his face. His blond hair was disheveled. Justin felt his lips quirk. Gabriel's letters always seemed anxious or weighed down. It was good to see him looking relaxed. As Justin approached, Sir Ranulf slipped from the seat next to Gabriel, smiling, and took his leave.

"You've vexed your watchdog," Gabriel drawled in greeting.

Justin felt his face heat. "He told me not to get drunk. As if I'm a child who's never tasted drink."

"Mm." Gabriel pressed his fingertips together. "Sweetgrass mead isn't the same as that watered ale you have in the capital."

"Which I know perfectly well." Justin tugged at his itchy collar. "I only want to relax a bit and celebrate being here. I haven't seen you since Midwinter."

"Ah, yes, and you've had a birthday since then, haven't you? Saints, you must be nearly ten by now." Gabriel's blue eyes sparked with mirth.

Justin kicked him under the table. "Ass. I'm fourteen." Oh. Of course Gabriel was teasing him. Justin held his breath to keep from sighing. Sometimes he didn't understand Gabriel's humor. Maybe it was because his cousin was four years older than him, but then again, it might be because he was so different from Brandon.

"Fourteen, of course. Well, your princeliness, how did you like your present?"

Justin lit up. "The huntmaster has been letting me train her myself. He says she'll make a fine hound if I treat her well. I named her Smoke," Justin said. "For her color. She sleeps at my feet every night."

His cousin looked pleased. "I'm glad your father let you keep her."

"Why wouldn't he? He says Jerol's hunting dogs are some of the finest in the kingdom."

"Smoke's from my favorite bitch's latest litter," Gabriel said. "If she turns out like her mother, you'll never meet a more devoted creature. Sweet-natured, too."

One of Justin's favorite things about Gabriel was how easily his cousin forgot Justin was the prince. Gabriel was handsome and clever, with a nice singing voice, and he was Justin's aunt's eldest son. Her only son, since the fever that had gone through five years ago. Gabriel was also second in line to the throne, unless Justin's parents had more children. That wouldn't happen, according to the Healers, because of the queen's falling ill during that same fever.

"You've a gaze that stretches across the plains," Gabriel said. He was leaning forward, studying Justin's face.

Justin sipped his mead. It was thick and tasted like the dry air and hot sun of the plains. "I was thinking about my parents." He looked Gabriel in the eye. "Do you think he'll set her aside?"

Surprise flickered through Gabriel's eyes and he frowned. "I don't know. He has to weigh the good of the entire kingdom against his regard for the queen and her love for you. Everyone respects Aunt Ariana, and I think sorrows for her. But some of the lords are putting pressure on your father. He's in a hard spot."

"What would you do?"

"Whatever my father thought I ought to do, I suppose." Gabriel's voice was low.

"That isn't a real answer," Justin accused.

Gabriel sighed. "It isn't a fair question, Jus. I love you too well to think of anything happening that would make your father need a second heir."

The polished stone of the floor suddenly seemed very interesting. Gabriel loved him? People were supposed to love their royals, of course, and people were supposed to love their cousins. But it was still strange to hear his cousin say the words so baldly.

Gabriel chuckled. "Ah, I forgot, you're fourteen. Love is a devil's word at that age, isn't it?" He tousled Justin's hair, which allowed Justin to glare at him. "Your father is a very fair man," Gabriel said after a moment. "I suppose he might think it fair to quietly send your mother here to live with us, while he marries again. But I hope I am wrong."

Justin chewed the side of his mouth. He loved his mother, though he knew what the other boys at the palace would have to say about that. But the law allowed for divorce, in certain cases, as long as it was done with the blessing of the Gods.

"You're thinking entirely too much," Gabriel said. "Come, let's get out. There are some pretty girls here who would desperately love to meet our prince, I think. And we have musicians set to play soon, and a bard for later."

Justin did his best to shake off his sudden gloom. Gabriel was right. His father would do what he thought best, and Justin could do nothing about it. Here at Jerol, Justin was free to think of other things.

"The prince seems almost a young man," Jon said. Brandon had dragged him into a corner of the feast hall, where the Prince's Knight had begun attacking a bottle of wine with a vengeance.

"He's only fourteen. Barely old enough for the king to begin talking about marriage alliances." Brandon's blue eyes were hooded.

"Saints, is he? Talking about an alliance, I mean?" Jon turned, startled, to look at the prince again. He was all height and knobbly joints, and there was a seriousness to his expression that made him look older than he was. Fourteen. Jon wondered if Brandon remembered what it was like to be fourteen. Then again, even eight years ago Brandon had acted a great deal older than he was. Growing up with a power-hungry mother who despised his father had not been easy.

Brandon grunted. "I think he's only doing it to make the lords stop harping on him about the queen. He'll never set her aside. He doesn't love her, nor she him, as best I can tell, but she's been a good queen. It drives the lords and clerics mad."

"Politics," Jon said. "Give me a sword in my hand and a song in my heart, and I'll happily live without politics all my days."

"Ha. Good fortune to you." Brandon took a long drink of his wine.

Jon turned to gaze at his friend. "You're absolutely foul, Bran. What's happened in the past four months to cause this?"

To his satisfaction, Brandon colored and looked down at the floor. He set his goblet aside. After a moment, he tilted his head back. "Things aren't easy in Laurenstat, Jon."

"You can't have thought it would be," Jon said.

Brandon shook his head. "It isn't the work. It's the politics, the frivolity, the--the--" He waved a hand. "All I ever wanted to do was use my sword in the king's service."

"Funny, I thought that's what the Elite Corps was about."

Brandon glared at him. "You know what I mean."

"I don't really." Jon kept his voice mild. "If you wanted to fight for the king, you could have stopped at taking your knighthood. You could have joined the army, for that matter. There's no need to join the Elite Corps if all you want to do is fight for the king." He tilted his head. "Unless you mean you never intended to love the prince. In which case, I suppose I do understand."

Brandon's shoulders heaved in an explosive sigh. "Has anyone ever told you how nosy you are?"

So it *was* the prince. The only thing Jon liked about court was the abundance of music and song. But it didn't require a keen observer to know Brandon's friendship with the prince made most courtiers jealous. Few understood a man whose greatest desire was neither power nor wealth, but merely to be useful to the prince.

Jon sipped his wine and remained silent. If Brandon wanted to elaborate, he would. It would do no good to push him. Brandon didn't deal well with emotions. If there was one thing Jon had learned over the years of their friendship, it was patience.

Finally Brandon sighed again. "The commander has started giving me more responsibility. Little things, at first, nothing unusual. But a few months ago--just after you and Lord Malnythe left the city--the commander sent some of us on an errand to the Druin River Valley. Things are unsettled down along the sand line, you know, and the king was worried about Lord Penbroshil. Sir Prysten Deireth was in command of the expedition, which was only proper. He's a good fighter, and utterly loyal. Stern, hard-working. He's the commander's second."

Jon nodded to show he was listening. In another corner of the hall, some musicians began playing. Jon scooted his chair a bit closer to Brandon's, pushing down a pang of regret for missed singing.

"Prysten pulled me aside our first day out, said he'd been ordered to bring me up. I was to be his second on the expedition. He wasn't friendly about it."

Jon grunted. He could see where that was going. The Prince's Knight being promoted ahead of a man who'd been in the Elite Corps longer would cause hard feelings.

"Exactly. He spent the whole expedition testing me. When we finally met up with Penbroshil's men, they said there was no trouble with the desert folk. You've heard the stories about the Druin River Valley. Well, there's truth enough in them. Marauding monsters of some sort had the Tekeyt and our folk alike in an uproar. Prysten said we'd look into it. I didn't think it was our job, but he overruled me."

Brandon was rubbing his leg, almost as if remembering a wound, but didn't seem aware of his movements.

"A band of haonggen had taken to preying on humans. But..." Brandon closed his eyes. "The haonggen had made their warren in the ruins of an old city. *Old* old, crumbled to stone ruins before our folk even crossed the ocean. They were using clubs and crude spears; you know how haonggen fight. My blade broke. *Broke*--a blade Justin gave me when I was knighted, made by the king's own swordmaker. And it shattered as if I'd come against the Dark King himself." He shuddered. "In the heat of the fight, I picked up a sword that was lying in the rubble." Brandon shrugged.

"I figured it would be rusted to nothing, probably break the first time I countered a blow. But it was... Well." He reached to his hip and bared a handbreadth of steel. "It's the finest blade I've ever seen. It saved my life, and it seems to have chosen me."

Jon frowned. "Chosen you."

Brandon shrugged. "I think this sword might be haunted. Sometimes I almost think it's talking to me in my head."

Talking to him? Jon sat forward. "Have you spoken to the clerics?" he asked, dropping his voice.

"Of course not. I don't want anyone to think I've gone mad." Brandon scowled at him. "Besides, the sword isn't even the point."

"But a haunted sword, Bran--"

"Leave it, Jon. I'll deal with it when I have to. The thing is, Prysten was wounded in the fight. We had a Healer with us, but even so, we didn't think he was going to pull through. We made it back to Port Kama, then we stopped there so he could recover." Brandon took a long drink of his wine and went on.

"We'd been there perhaps a week when General Hasha himself called for me. I was to go on to Laurenstat alone. He wouldn't say why. I spent the whole trip wondering if Godfric was going to have me dismissed, or if the commander was displeased with me, or what."

Brandon ran a hand over his face. "When I arrived, the commander said I would be his new second, and began training me. By the time the rest of my group got back, Prysten hale and strong again, I'd replaced him. He won't even look at me now, unless he has to. And it's a load of horse shit. I'm good, I won't deny that, won't even pretend. But Prysten's got at least a decade on me, and he's been in the Elite Corps all this time. If they're promoting me just because I'm friends with Justin--"

"And now you're in charge of the excursion here," Jon interrupted. "And Prysten isn't with you, I take it."

Brandon shook his head. "It's made things difficult. More difficult than usual. A lot of these men are Prysten's friends, you know. They all follow orders, but..."

Jon nodded. "Not an easy situation."

"No." Brandon barked a laugh. "Not an easy situation."

Jon rubbed his jaw. "At least the king must trust you. He wouldn't give you this sort of assignment if he didn't trust you. Not even for the prince's best friend."

Brandon snorted. "Some comfort."

CHAPTER TWO

Gabriel surprised himself by being the first of his friends to arrive at the breakfast table the next morning. The Prince's Knight was probably up and about somewhere; Gabriel wasn't sure Brandon Shrike ever slept. But Jon and Ranulf were both early risers, and Gabriel had never been fond of mornings, so he'd expected to see them, at least, awake before him.

He snagged the arm of the next serving maid he saw and asked. She curtsied, looking far too bright-eyed for the hour. "Lord Shrike came through and took bread and a slice of meat, my lord. Your lady mother is still abed, and the prince."

"What about Jon or Ranulf?"

"Is Sir Destry home, my lord? I haven't seen him, nor Sir Jon."

Gabriel sighed. He'd hoped for time to speak with Ranulf this morning. They'd had time for a hasty greeting the day before, but not long enough to discuss the matter that weighed on Gabriel's mind. It would be difficult to avoid Brandon Shrike all day, with the way Shrike was dogging Justin's heels like a shepherd. "Thank you, Kamisa," Gabriel said, realizing the serving girl was still waiting for him to speak. "Bring me something hot and strong to drink, would you? My head is still in a fog."

She smiled impishly at him. "Too much mead last night, my lord. And you setting an example for the prince, la." Giggling, she twirled away from him to fetch his drink.

Gabriel shook his head, his lips curling in pleasure. Perhaps being duke of Jerol someday wouldn't be so bad. His father's people liked him, or seemed to, and Gabriel did love his home. Before the fever he had hoped, perhaps foolishly, his father would agree to have Chid or Arthi as his heir, freeing Gabriel to join the clergy, where he could study and pray to his heart's content.

"The Just Goddess gives each man his place," he murmured, tearing a piece off his bread. "It ill becomes a man to refute her gift."

"They say talking to yourself is a sign of madness," said an acerbic voice. Even before Gabriel lifted his head, he knew the Prince's Knight had found him.

"That would explain a lot of things," he said, giving Brandon a rueful smile. To his pleasure, Brandon chuckled as he took a seat down the table from Gabriel.

"You've quite a place here, Lord Malnythe. I'd seen the eastern plains, of course, but I'd never been so far west of the Coastal Highway. This vast emptiness..." Brandon shook his head. "It's something to see."

"Ah, but it isn't empty, not if you look closely enough," Gabriel said. "There are few trees, it's true, but the bushes and tall grass are home to birds of all kinds, and there are fleetdeer and hares. And the horses...Saints, those horses. I've loved the herds all my life."

Brandon had one eyebrow raised, the corner of his mouth pulled to one side, as he studied Gabriel. Gabriel wondered if had spoken too poetically for Brandon's taste. Well, if he had, so what? It only proved what he had claimed for years--he was no warrior. He was a poet, a thinker, a dreamer. Not a fighter, for all that he could wield a sword.

"One thing I'll say for it, all that open terrain makes security easier." Brandon pulled an apple from the bowl and took a bite.

"And that, I suppose, makes clear the differences between your outlook on life and mine," Gabriel said. He wasn't sure whether to be amused or depressed. Brandon just grunted. Gabriel was debating if he should explain when Kamisa returned, bearing a metal pot and two mugs.

"I saw Lord Shrike join you, my lord, so I brought enough for two," she said. "Freshly brewed, and strong as you like it."

Gabriel thanked her with a smile and began pouring.

"Is that your way of saying you refuse to help me protect the prince's life?" Brandon asked.

Gabriel jerked the pot upwards to keep from spilling the hot drink. "If I have something to tell you, I shall tell you straight out, Lord Shrike," he said. "I was only making conversation."

He reached for Brandon's mug, but the other man's calloused hand closed hard around his wrist. "Then tell me straight out, Lord Malnythe."

Gabriel locked Brandon's gaze, his stomach churning. This was what he had wanted to put off another day. If he had discussed it with Ranulf instead of allowing himself to be distracted by all the greetings and business of settling his guests...

"Spit it out, Malnythe. It's a short word." Brandon's voice was low. He'd already made up his mind that Gabriel was going to say no.

"Of course I'm going to join the Elite Corps. I am eighteen, and my father's sole heir." Gabriel heard the words fall from his mouth but didn't quite believe them himself, so he supposed Brandon could be forgiven for the skeptical laugh he uttered.

"You could have joined two years ago. You *should* have joined two years ago."

Gabriel jerked his wrist out of Brandon's grip. "I am sure you will understand I felt my father had more need of me here than the prince did in Laurenstat, at that time. Which I explained two years ago, as I recall." Saints, had he just agreed to become an Elite Corps warrior? The bread he'd eaten seemed stuck in his throat.

Brandon tilted his head. There was a gleam in his eyes Gabriel didn't like. "Well. I suppose that's in the past. We'll tell your cousin the good news today, and when I take the Corps members out for our exercise, you can join us."

Gabriel was going to throw up. "Exercise...what?"

"We're having a mock battle to give the Elite Corps men some experience in this terrain. That captain of yours, Hakin, I think it was? He suggested we ride out south and west. Says there's a mountain or something where we'll have varied landscape."

"Look, you're not here to start training me, Shrike, you're here to keep my cousin safe while he visits me. I have duties here." That was a lie. Everything here would probably run just as smoothly without him present. More smoothly, in fact. Their chatelaine was more than capable, and Captain Hakin and Savona took care of security without any help from Gabriel.

Brandon tsked. "You're going to have to get better at taking orders, Malnythe."

Gabriel was at a loss. He hadn't even meant to join the Elite Corps! If he'd been able to talk to Ranulf, he could surely have found some way to refuse without insulting Shrike or disappointing Justin. Or his father. In truth, Duke Frewyn was far more likely to be disappointed than Justin was. Justin seemed never to blame anyone for their weaknesses. He was a charitable lad.

Brandon made a disgusted noise in his throat. "Oh, fine. Have it your way. You can call this your last bit of leisure. But you'll be ready to ride back to Laurenstat with us when we go, or I'll know why not."

Gabriel had not been the sort of boy who practiced salutes, but he thought he managed to inject irony into the salute he gave Brandon just then. At least, it soured Brandon's expression further.

Gabriel thought he could call that a victory. Of sorts.

"You did what?" Ranulf turned from where he had been leaning on the stall door to stare at Gabriel in shock. "My lord--"

"Don't," Gabriel muttered. The stable was empty for the moment, aside from the two of them and the Elite Corps horses. There was no need for formality between them.

Ranulf fell silent, his mouth hanging open. He'd grown a beard sometime in the last year. It was trimmed close around his mouth, emphasizing, rather than hiding, his strong jawline. His blue eyes were troubled. "Gabriel," he said, lowering his voice, "Gabriel, why? I know it isn't what you want. We--we would have thought of something, some way to keep Brandon from judging you for it."

Gabriel shook his head and looked away. His heart hurt, sometimes, when he looked at Ranulf. There was so much about Ranulf that Gabriel...not envied, not exactly, because he would never wish to take away Ranulf's easy self-possession. But he wished he knew how to emulate it. "I think," he said at last, "Brandon Shrike would judge me wanting even if I died saving Justin's life. But I couldn't stand the derision in his eyes. He'd already decided I was going to say no. He--" Gabriel laughed unhappily. "He probably even knew what he was going to say back."

Ranulf's mouth turned down. "He's a good man, Gabriel. I know he's hard, he expects a lot, but... He only wants to serve the prince."

"I know." That was the hell of it. Gabriel believed that. He just didn't think he would ever be the sort of man Brandon Shrike respected.

"Let me take your place again, as I have these past two years," Ranulf said. He lowered himself to one knee, tilting his head back to look up at Gabriel. "You know I'm your man. I swore it then, and I swear it again now. All I have done in the past two years, I have done in your name, for your honor. And I'll do that again. I will make Lord Shrike see you as I see you."

Gabriel smiled and reached out to pluck a blade of straw from Ranulf's brown hair. "I doubt anyone will ever see me as you do, Ran," he murmured. "You know me better than anyone, and you're too kind to judge me wanting."

Several stalls down, a horse thumped its feed bucket. Ranulf looked in that direction. When he turned his gaze back up to Gabriel, his expression was warm. "I taught you so much, if I thought you wanting, it would be a reflection on my own skills." He chuckled. "I still remember the boy who joined us for missions among the Shallans, the boy I shared a cloak with and taught to ride without a saddle."

Gabriel felt his face heat. "You were a good teacher," he muttered. He seized Ranulf's shoulders and hauled him to his feet. "Get up. I know you meant to take my place permanently, but it's out of my hands. I'll make certain that you can stay on."

"Serving in the Elite Corps alongside you would please me well," Ranulf said. "As long as it didn't force me to watch you sink into misery as you shaped yourself into a warrior instead of a philosopher."

Gabriel's lips trembled and he pressed them together to hide his current misery. He shook his head and squeezed Ranulf's shoulder. "I should tell Jon." He heard the roughness in his voice and knew Ranulf would call him on it if he didn't go quickly.

Ranulf sighed. "Gabriel..." But he trailed off and shook his head. "I pledged myself to you years ago, and I stand by that. Only command me, my lord."

Gabriel nodded and forced a smile, then strode out of the stables without looking back.

Justin frowned into his cup. His aunt had been in a foul mood all through dinner, and finally she had announced she was retiring for the evening. Justin had expected the stilted atmosphere to lighten when she left, but instead Gabriel had fallen into a gloom. Sir Destry was picking at his dessert and

Brandon had abandoned eating and dedicated himself to the mead.

There were half a dozen of Jerol's wealthier tenants dining with them, as well as several household members. This wasn't the proper place to clear the air. But Justin had run out of polite topics of conversation, and he was beginning to feel cranky himself.

One of Gabriel's hounds was sleeping between Gabriel's and Justin's chairs. It snored faintly. Justin shifted his foot over until he could feel the warmth of the hound's side through his breeches. When would this interminable dinner end?

At last Gabriel stood and said a few polite words to the guests, then excused himself. His departure loosened the tension in the room, and three of his tenants approached him on their way out. Justin traced a finger around the top of his cup and watched his cousin's posture change as he devoted his attention to each vassal in turn.

Justin knew Gabriel didn't think of himself as a charismatic leader or a warrior. Justin suspected that was mostly because Uncle Frewyn was so hard on Gabriel. As the king's highest advisor and the most powerful nobleman in the kingdom, Frewyn had a great deal of responsibility; he seemed to think Gabriel should wish to step into his role at some point--yet he also seemed to think Gabriel would not be capable in that role.

As Justin watched Gabriel's face light up during a conversation with a beekeeper, he thought his cousin would surprise them all. The woman responded to Gabriel's attention by relaxing and smiling back at him, her own expression animated. They were too far away for their conversation to carry, but the tenant was clearly charmed by Gabriel. Whatever her concern, it had melted away.

The second man greeted Gabriel with an outstretched hand and a smile. Gabriel treated him the same as he had the woman, and the man nodded. They exchanged a few more words, then Gabriel pointed the man in the direction of the chatelaine.

"He'll be good at this," Justin said softly. Sir Destry, who had just pushed his chair back, glanced over at him. Gabriel's hound stretched and trotted out from under the table to follow her master.

"Your highness?"

"My cousin," Justin replied, smiling. He glanced at where Gabriel was bowing over an older woman's hand. Justin supposed she must be a village elder of some sort. Her expression was serious. "He loves these people. And I think they love him. He listens to them, and they sense that. It makes them trust him. He will be good at this, when he succeeds Duke Frewyn."

Sir Destry's smile was quick and fierce. "I believe the prince sees keenly," he murmured.

Justin grinned back at him. "You love him a great deal, don't you?" He managed not to stumble over the word, though Gabriel was right; 'love' came only haltingly to the tongue of a fourteen-year-old, prince or no.

"I have all my life," Destry replied. "I would have served in the Elite Corps on my own choice, but I have been honored to serve in Lord Gabriel's place, at Lord Gabriel's will."

Justin tilted his head. "You have been," he repeated.

Destry flushed. "I should not have said that, highness."

"No, I think you meant to," Justin said. He studied Destry, seeing the flush spread higher along the knight's cheekbones. "You're angry with him."

Destry ducked his head. "Not angry, my prince. Merely..." He paused, his gaze landing on Gabriel's form and then flitting away. "Merely sad. It is of no import."

Justin raised an eyebrow. "It is the prerogative of a prince to decide for himself what is of import, Sir Destry." He stood. "Come, let us walk, you and I, and speak more privately of what saddens you."

"Prince Justin--" Destry began, then bowed. "As you wish."

Justin led the way out of the hall and headed for a small courtyard that had trees and a nice place to sit. He liked Destry.

The man was several years older than Justin, close to Brandon's age, he thought, but he always treated Justin with a friendly courtesy. Whatever was making Destry sad when he looked at Gabriel, Justin wanted to know about it.

Justin had learned patience through his training, both in the law and in the sword. He did not speak until he and Destry were protected by courtyard walls from eavesdroppers. It gave him the opportunity to observe the tension in Destry's shoulders and the sidelong looks the man gave him. Strange, in the normally self-assured knight.

"Well then," Justin said. "What saddens you when you look at my cousin, Sir Destry?"

There was less light in the courtyard, as twilight slipped her cloak across the sky, but he could see the blush darken Destry's face. "Highness, I...I would normally say it is not my place to speak of such things..." Destry trailed off.

Justin flashed him a smile. "Normally, of course," he agreed. "But since your prince asks you to speak..."

Destry bowed. "Gabriel has told Lord Shrike he will be joining the Elite Corps when we return to Laurenstat." He scratched his beard. "Until today, I believed I had been appointed to the Elite Corps for the entire course of my life, to serve in Gabriel's place."

Ah, that explained so much. Aunt Elna's mood, Gabriel's unhappiness, even Brandon's seeming intent to get drunk tonight. It was no secret Gabriel, though adequately accomplished as a fighter, was no true warrior at heart. Nevertheless, Justin had to be sure he understood. "And you have no desire to leave the Elite Corps and return to your life from before?"

Destry cleared his throat. "It is true I would be happy to serve you until I die, highness. But that is not what saddens me; my lord has said he will ensure my appointment for me."

"Mm. Then you are sad because you know my cousin does not love war."

"That is the right of it, highness."

Justin nodded. "What would you have me do, Ranulf?"

"I spoke only because you asked it." Destry shook his head. "I make no request of you, highness. I know it is right for Gabriel to wish to serve. I...I only wish he could serve in a manner that would not--" Destry broke off and looked away.

Justin waited, but Destry didn't continue. Frowning, Justin tapped his fingers against the stone wall of the courtyard fountain. "You think service in the Elite Corps would...what? Break his spirit? Speak openly with me, Ranulf. I love my cousin well, and I would see him happy."

"As would I," Destry whispered. He bowed his head, pressing his fingers against his eyes. "Prince Justin, Gabriel pushes himself to be the son Duke Frewyn requires. He has sacrificed so much to please his father, and he will have to sacrifice more. He wished to join the clergy, did you know?" When Justin nodded, the knight continued, "And now he will have to marry and sire heirs. He has learned the sword, but he does not love it. And I...I think he did not mean to marry. It seems very hard he should also be forced to fight and kill in the king's name, when it goes against his very nature." Destry's voice had been growing stronger. Now he seemed to realize it; he coughed and looked away again.

Justin sighed. "It does seem hard on him," he murmured. "I will think on this and come to a decision before we leave Jerol. You have the word of a prince on it, Ranulf."

Destry stared at him. The surprise on his face made him look younger, and Justin smiled. "I told you, I love my cousin, and I know him. There are many ways he can serve me without reshaping his character. I will find a solution."

Destry bowed so deeply Justin had the impulse to look over his shoulder, in case his father had suddenly appeared from the capital. A prince, even a crown prince, didn't rate such a bow. It made Justin's throat feel tight.

He put his hands on Destry's shoulders and straightened him. "I must speak with Gabriel. Will you excuse me, Sir Destry?"

"My prince." Destry saluted, and Justin left him there. It was time to speak with his cousin

"You might have told me what you were planning."

Gabriel had come to his study to be alone. He'd been standing at the window, looking out into the darkness, for so long his joints had stiffened. The fire was dying.

Prince Justin stood in the doorway, his hands on his hips. His eyes were shadowed, and Gabriel had a sudden vision of the king he would become. He sighed. "You're angry with me."

Scowling, Justin came inside and shut the door. "Not angry," he said. "Sad."

Gabriel raised his eyebrows.

"Disappointed." Justin tilted his head. "All right, perhaps a bit exasperated." He knelt in front of the hearth and poked at the fire. "You don't want to be a member of the Elite Corps. You and I both know that. For that matter, Brandon knows it. He doesn't understand, of course, but that isn't important."

Gabriel huffed and poured them both a goblet of wine. "It won't look good if I neglect my duty."

"Not everyone of noble birth goes through the Elite Corps," Justin said. "I can think of half a dozen heirs around your age who haven't applied or been invited."

"And are any of them the only living son of the king's advisor, heir to the most powerful duke in the central part of the kingdom?" Gabriel drank deeply and turned back to the window.

"Perhaps I shall make you the head chronicler of my reign after I am crowned," Justin replied. "Perhaps I shall create a new position for you--chief researcher of...of..."

"Of the best ways to disappoint one's father?" Gabriel didn't bother smoothing the bitterness from his voice. "Of the barbs most likely to prick the Prince's Knight's skin?"

"Don't." Justin's voice was tight. "You have great value to me, Gabriel. And to others. Can you truly be ignorant of what Ranulf Destry feels for you?"

Gabriel snorted, though his chest tightened. No, he was not ignorant of it. He did not understand it, and he thanked the Gods every day for it, but he was not ignorant of it. "Ranulf sees only the best in people."

"And you see only the worst in yourself!" Justin snapped. "Stop being such a fool!"

Gabriel shrugged and drained his glass. He could see distant campfires out on the plains. The Shallans had accepted his hospitality for the first night after Justin arrived, but the Horse Clans were never comfortable inside stone walls. They were a largely nomadic people, and preferred their tent walls and campfires.

Justin sighed explosively. "You are not going to be in the Elite Corps, Gabriel. I can't allow it."

"You would do the discourtesy of denying me?" All at once, Gabriel felt incredibly tired. Why was Justin doing this? It would look like Gabriel had regretted his decision and gone begging his cousin to wield his power on his behalf.

"Shut up," Justin muttered. "I'm going away. I'll see you tomorrow."

Gabriel heard the door open and close, but he didn't turn away from the window. He pressed his forehead against the glass. He could endure the Elite Corps. For noble heirs, it was usually only a handful of years, however long it took them to inherit. He had adjusted to the idea of being the Duke of Jerol. He could adjust to this. Couldn't he?

He closed his eyes.

CHAPTER THREE

Justin shoved his book away from him and rubbed his eyes. This was his third day cooped up in the library with Gabriel's books, and he was beginning to feel restless. He enjoyed learning, and he was expected to be familiar with the laws and customs of all the peoples of his kingdom. But he had been looking forward to spending time with Gabriel, and he hadn't reckoned on having some dispute come up that required the lord's attention.

Aunt Elna didn't have much to do with the governing of Jerol. She liked music and embroidery, and Uncle Frewyn obliged her. It had always fallen to Frewyn's sons to take part in the government. Now Gabriel was the only son left, Justin imagined his responsibilities were even more demanding, especially with Duke Frewyn currently busy at court.

Still, Justin would have been happy to accompany Gabriel and the Just Goddess' cleric to Winsside for the adjudication. It would have been fun, but it would also have been educational, as he'd argued when he tried to join them. Brandon had held firm it was not part of their plan, and therefore unsafe. Justin's temper had flared, Brandon had roared back in response, and the prince had not spoken to his knight for the past two days.

"Honestly," he muttered, running his fingernail along a seam in the table. "I know he's supposed to protect me, but this is ridiculous." Jerol was the most stable fief in the kingdom. If Brandon didn't trust him to stay out of trouble here, how low was his opinion of the prince?

"You're sulking," Justin told himself. "It's unbecoming of a prince. It's churlish. It would displease the Just Goddess. We are to accept the justice She sends without complaint."

The lecture didn't make him feel any better. He shoved his chair away from the table and left the library. It was past lunch time, and he should have eaten with everyone else, instead of inconveniencing the kitchen staff, but he hadn't wanted to see Brandon. His actions embarrassed him now, but he still wasn't eager to spend time with anyone. It was so tempting to steal out to the stables and escape his keepers for a while.

He'd almost worked up the determination to do just that by the time he reached the ground floor of the manor. Avoiding the main passages, he slipped into a servants' hallway on the stable side of the house. Just as he stepped outside, he felt a hand clamp on his shoulder.

"As I recall, one of our rules was you wouldn't leave the manor house without telling someone." Brandon's voice was surprisingly mild.

Justin pressed a hand against his chest, embarrassed his heart had given such a jump. He hadn't been *afraid*. Just startled. He let Brandon tug him around, preparing himself for another argument. To his shock, Brandon was smiling. It happened so rarely it always made Justin smile back. He caught himself at it and tried to wipe the expression away, but Brandon had already seen.

"I'm sorry, Jus. I've been a proper ass, haven't I?"

Justin folded his arms across his chest. Saints take him, it was unfair for Brandon to use his charm. "I confess, I'd never taken you for such a prig." He made his voice as severe as he could.

Brandon ducked his head in mock repentance. "An accusation that wounds me."

"I'm bored as the grave, Brandon. Let's at least go for a ride. Or you could show me some of your fancy swordwork. I promised Master Cronai I would keep my hand in this month."

"Have you been drilling?"

"Every morning," Justin snapped. "It's been one of the few enjoyable things about this visit."

"Now that's uncharitable." Brandon's brows drew down. "Your cousin has gone out of his way to make you feel comfortable and welcome. You shouldn't begrudge him his duties."

Justin sighed. "You're right, I didn't mean that. But I truly am bored, Bran. *Please*, can we spar or something?"

Brandon's expression relaxed. "All right. If you can disarm me, I'll even teach you that trick I told you about."

They split the next hour between drills and practice bouts, though Justin never managed to disarm his best friend. It stung his pride, but he promised himself when he was twenty-two, he wouldn't let anyone disarm him, either. It just proved he'd chosen the best warrior in the kingdom to be his personal knight-protector.

Gabriel returned while they were in the practice ring. He looked tired and dusty, but he smiled warmly at Justin when he saw them. "Fine form," he called, approaching. "I can see you've all been having more fun than I."

Justin glared at him, which made him laugh.

"All right," Gabriel said. "I'm sorry I had to leave you behind, cousin. I'll make it up to you, I swear."

"You'd better. That Bard of Kinsten wasn't a very good writer." Justin had labored over the dry collection of Shallan legends for half a day, wondering how anyone could make blood feuds sound boring.

Gabriel hooted. "Saints have mercy, you didn't spend too much time on that one, did you? I told you the Tanarae was much more interesting."

Justin turned his back on him. "That's the only reason I might consider forgiving you. Now go away, we haven't finished this drill set."

He could hear Gabriel chuckling behind him as he attacked Brandon with new ferocity. It wasn't good to fight when you'd lost your temper, so he tried to tamp down his rekindled anger. Brandon got in a hard thump against his ribs, reminding him *why* it wasn't good to fight when you'd lost your temper. That settled him, and he began striking with more precision and less force.

When their last bout was finished, he heard clapping behind him. He turned and discovered Gabriel had never left. His cousin brought over a water skin.

"Your skill has improved by miles since the last time I saw you fight. And you were already dazzling with a blade."

Justin was glad he was already hot, or he might have blushed. "I work hard at it, that's all."

Gabriel shook his head. "That's not all. You enjoy it, too. I can see the delight in your whole body when you strike the forms perfectly. You're gifted."

Justin shrugged and wiped his face. When he looked up again, Brandon was studying Gabriel, who seemed oblivious to Brandon's scrutiny as he held out the water skin.

Justin drank deeply and poured some over his head before offering it to Brandon. It distracted his best friend from his cousin, which Justin suspected was a good thing.

The great hall seemed merry at dinner that night. Gabriel had enjoyed his time with the adjudicator, and Winsside was a pleasant town. The innkeeper made famous apple tarts worth the half-day's ride from Jerol on their own. But throughout his errand to Winsside, Gabriel had felt guilty he'd been forced to leave Justin. He understood that Brandon had felt it best for his cousin to stay behind, but he didn't agree there was a need for it.

He did his best to make up for his absence by telling Justin about the trip in great detail, setting the case of the disputed water rights before him and asking what Justin would have decided in his place. Justin asked thoughtful questions about the scarcity of water on the plains and local traditions concerning water use, then made the same decision Gabriel had--the two herders in question would have to share the water, both of them traveling to the spring rather than diverting the water closer to their flocks. Justin seemed pleased he and Gabriel agreed, but he grew quieter after that.

After the meal was finished, Gabriel brought out a gaming board and set up one of the popular layouts of Strat. Justin opted to have Brandon and Ranulf play against him and Gabriel, and they spent several hours moving pieces back and forth over the contested territory. It was late in the evening when Brandon stretched, yawning.

"We should be off to bed." He nudged Ranulf, who had his chin propped on a hand, studying the board. "Stay up if you like, but I'll laugh if you fall asleep on your horse and get dumped."

"Sparrow would never dump me," Ranulf said, smiling. He looked over at Gabriel. "We ride out in the morning for our exercise. Perhaps we could persuade you to leave the board set up until we return?"

Gabriel shrugged. "I don't mind. There's no getting out of the box you're in, but if you want further punishment, I won't object."

Brandon was snickering when Justin said, "I want to go with you."

Gabriel pursed his lips and glanced at his cousin. That idea wouldn't go over well with Brandon, if the idea of a short errand to Winsside had been refused. But Justin was sitting very straight, his jaw jutting out. Saints help them, this was going to be unpleasant.

"Not a chance." Brandon's tone was dismissive, which would only make Justin dig his heels in.

"I am the prince," Justin said. "Which means the Elite Corps is my bodyguard, as well as my father's. But I must also know how to fight alongside the Elite Corps. I will not behave like a shivering coward, to hide behind a wall of men."

"This is neither the time nor the place," Brandon began, but Justin cut him off.

"I bode by your decision about Winsside because that was part of Gabriel's duties, not my own. But the Elite Corps is part of my duties. You will not deny me the right to perform my duty, Baronet Shrike."

Gabriel met Ranulf's eyes; they both wished to be elsewhere. He lowered his gaze to the game board and pretended he couldn't hear the argument.

"Then you would deny me the right to perform *my* duty, Prince Justin?" Brandon's voice was cold. Justin had hurt him, Gabriel thought with an inward wince.

"Your duty is to command this group of Elite Corps," Justin retorted. "It is also to safeguard me, which you can hardly do if I am not with you. I fail to see how I am denying you anything."

"You will be well protected inside manor walls. I will not countenance any other idea. Justin, you are the crown prince, the sole heir to the kingdom. When are you going to see you are too precious to risk?"

Justin went rigid next to Gabriel. "I am going."

Brandon's hand crashed down on the table. "YOU WILL STAY HERE!" he roared. Gabriel jumped, but he was saved any embarrassment by the knowledge Justin had jumped too. The prince fell silent, glaring mutinously at his knight-protector. A moment later he shoved his chair back with a clatter and ran from the room.

A long silence followed Justin's departure. Finally Ranulf cleared his throat and picked up the chair from where it had fallen. Brandon covered his face with one hand, breathing heavily. Gabriel sighed and stood.

"Ranulf, I thank you for a game well played," he murmured. Ranulf gave him a faint smile and inclined his torso in a slight bow.

"It was my pleasure to let you beat me," he joked. It allowed Gabriel to laugh.

"Let me," he said, shaking his head. "We'll see in a day or two if you can make good on that statement. Off to bed with you, impertinent man."

Ranulf went, his step light. Gabriel was pleased he had managed that. He squared his shoulders. Now for the hard task--Brandon would just as likely break Gabriel's nose as hear him. Gabriel turned to look at Brandon Shrike.

The Prince's Knight had allowed his hands to fall to his sides, and he was looking blankly at the game board. "I have never met such a willful, misguided brat as that boy," he muttered.

Gabriel's lips pulled to one side as he suppressed a smile. "I suspect you have forgotten what it is like to be fourteen, Lord Shrike," he suggested.

Brandon looked up at him, his blue eyes so icy they seemed gray. "When I was fourteen, my mother had disinherited me and I was serving as Prince's Page, Malnythe." His shoulders heaved in a sigh. "He has never been biddable, but lately it seems we argue as much as we speak to each other. Can he not understand I have his best interests at heart?"

"I suspect, in his better moments, he knows that very well." Gabriel tapped his fingers on the table. "Forbidding him to accompany you..." He cleared his throat. "Perhaps it would have been better done in private."

"He brought it up!"

"Peace." Gabriel tried to smile. "I was here. I know what happened. I am not faulting you. I am only suggesting...a prince has a great deal of pride anyway. A prince at fourteen has an overwhelming amount of pride. And said pride is, unfortunately, quite fragile."

Brandon scowled at him, but he finally sighed. "Ah, he'll cool off. I'll talk to him when we get back."

Gabriel's smile faltered. "It wouldn't hurt to let Justin see even strong men, whom he admires, are well-suited to humble themselves from time to time."

Brandon's brows drew together. "You're a blasted nuisance, Gabriel Malnythe."

The Prince's Knight stood and strode out of the hall.

———————✕———————

Jon crossed the courtyard, exchanging greetings with Elite Corps warriors and servants as they prepared the Corps for departure. He didn't bother asking the whereabouts of their commander. He knew which office Captain Savona had assigned for Brandon's use, and he knew Brandon well enough to be certain his friend would be there, brooding.

Jon paused in the office door. Brandon stood with his back to the door, bent over the desk. His shoulders were bowed. Jon didn't think he was imagining the exhaustion in the lines of Brandon's posture.

"You can stop lurking and come inside." Brandon's tone was acerbic.

Jon chuckled ruefully. "You've the ears of a cat," he said. He came inside and eased the door shut behind him.

"Instinct," Brandon said. Jon saw one hand brush the hilt of that cursed sword. Then Brandon dropped his hands to his side and turned. "What brings you here?"

Jon shrugged. "Am I not allowed to bid a friend farewell?"

Brandon laughed, his shoulders relaxing visibly. "Aye, except if it were an innocent farewell, you'd have come in loudly and not crept up to the door like a mouse checking the housecat's vigilance."

"Caught out." Jon sighed. "You know me too well."

"So what is it, then?" Brandon turned back to his desk and began rolling a map. "Here to chide me for badgering Lord Malnythe into the Corps?"

Jon's stomach dropped. Had Gabriel decided for the Corps, then? He swallowed. "I didn't realize you had." He knew his voice sounded too casual.

Brandon grunted. "Doesn't tell you everything after all, eh?"

Jon clenched his fingers, and then forced them to relax. "Nor should he. My father is a gentleman, but Lord Malnythe is still my better."

Brandon rounded on him, his fist wrinkling the map roll. "You're worth ten of him, Jon," he said fiercely. "And never let him tell you otherwise."

Jon sighed. That had backfired. "He never has," he said. "In fact he often tells me I'm better with a blade."

"And with your judgment," Brandon muttered. "Very well, what is it you want, if you aren't here to plead for your precious Gabriel's freedom?"

Jon frowned. Could Brandon be jealous of Gabriel's friendship with Jon? It seemed unlike him--but then again, Gabriel was skilled at pleasing people, and Brandon was anything but. Perhaps that grated. He shook his head, dismissing the thought.

"I'm here because I'm concerned about that sword of yours," he said. It was true, as far as it went, even if it wasn't the whole truth. He was also here because Gabriel had told him about the quarrel between Brandon and Prince Justin, and that worried Jon. Worried them both, actually.

"Damn it, I told you to leave it be!" Brandon flared. "I'll sort it out when I have to. Would you have me protect the prince without a weapon?"

"You're leaving the prince here with us, I hear," Jon replied, taking refuge in the imperturbable rumble he often used to quell belligerence. If Brandon were paying attention, he would realize Jon was upset, but Jon suspected his friend was too on edge to notice.

Brandon paced across the office, one hand pressed against the sword hilt. To Jon's dismay, Brandon didn't even seem to know he was doing it. "I have to. I'm tasked with protecting him. This exercise is to give us practice drilling in unfamiliar territory, and I can't keep him safe in unfamiliar territory."

"I would suggest there is no one more qualified than you to keep him safe." Jon folded his arms across his chest. He was a burly, broad-shouldered man, and he knew the stance made him look like a small mountain. He had learned early on in his growth to look intimidating so he could avoid fighting. "You could ask him for a new blade to replace the one that broke."

"I can't." Brandon rubbed a hand over his face. "I cared poorly for it. He deserves better of me."

"Perhaps the blade was flawed," Jon suggested. "It isn't your fa--"

"The blade was perfect!" Brandon snapped. "Let it go, Jonathan. Serodyn will more than suffice."

Serodyn. Jon shivered. He didn't like the sound of the name any more than he liked the blade itself.

"And how does the young prince feel about being left behind?" he asked.

"He'll get over it," Brandon said. He shoved the map into a leather case and tied it closed. "I'll make it up to him when I get back."

"How?" Jon demanded. "By bringing him back a present? Perhaps you could find a blade to match yours for the prince."

Brandon paced closer to him, fists clenched. "If anyone but you spoke to me so," he began, and then sighed. "Saints, I'm tired." He lifted a hand to scrub it through his hair, and Jon saw that his elbow had been pressed against the sword hilt. The more Jon saw of this blade, then less easy he felt about it. "I cry you mercy, Jon. I will feel better if Justin is here. I may not like your Lord Malnythe much, but I trust him and his warriors and his keep to protect Justin better than I could out on the open plains."

Jon took a few breaths before reaching out to place a hand on Brandon's shoulder. "I understand," he said, gentling his voice. "I am only afraid that the prince will not."

Brandon's expression was bleak. "I don't need him to understand or like it. I only need him to obey. He'll cool down while I'm away. He's a good lad. By the time I get back and talk to him, he'll have figured out why I did it."

Jon didn't think that was the case, but he had argued as much as he cared to. He clapped Brandon on the shoulder and stepped back. "I hope your exercise goes as you want it to," he said. "I wish I were free to observe. They seem like a well-disciplined group of warriors."

"They are." A rare smile lit Brandon's face. "For all that they don't care for me, they're a joy to work with. Smart and experienced and skilled beyond all others."

CHAPTER FOUR

Justin glanced over his shoulder one last time. If he were caught now, he would never get out of the keep. Gabriel would be disappointed and lock him in his room, and when Brandon returned, he would shout. Justin was tired of shouting.

The darkened hallway was empty. Justin slipped out the door into the courtyard. The Elite Corps had a day's head start, but he'd needed to wait until nightfall. Nearly everyone was at dinner now. Justin had sent a note to Gabriel, pleading a headache. He'd had a tray carried to his room. As soon as it arrived, he'd scooped the food into a bag and headed for the stable. He'd already left a bag of clothes in his horse's stall, and the bedroll he'd carried all the way from the capital.

There was still a faint line of orange on the horizon, but stars were twinkling overhead. Justin smiled up at the Scale and thought of the time Brandon had sworn to be his justice. "Aren't you afraid of blasphemy?" Justin had asked, but Brandon had only smiled. Life had been simpler then, when they were both younger and Justin hadn't felt the need to prove himself to Brandon all the time.

He shook himself and glanced around the courtyard before ducking into the stables. Time to move. Gabriel would probably check on him after dinner, and Justin wanted to be well away before then. Gabriel knew the land better than Justin, but given enough of a head start, Justin should be all right.

He unlatched Mist's stall door and nearly dropped his pack when he realized someone was lurking in the shadows inside. "Who are you?" he demanded, his hand dropping to his sword hilt.

"I thought you'd never get here," Gabriel said.

Justin recoiled. "What are you--I thought--I--"

Gabriel had a pleasant laugh. "You thought I was at dinner, and you would have plenty of time for a head start. And no, I'm not going to drag you up to your rooms and lock you in. It's a tempting notion when I consider that Shrike will have my head for this. But the idea doesn't sit well with me. So I'm opting for the next best option."

Justin watched him suspiciously.

Gabriel shrugged. "I'm coming with you."

They rode in silence for the first several miles. Gabriel had expected more of an argument, so he was grateful Justin was only sulking. Or so he thought, until Justin finally chuckled.

"All afternoon, I thought I was putting one over on you," he said.

Gabriel peered through the darkness at his cousin. "You might have been, if I hadn't gotten so much experience with Chid and Arthi." He coughed. "And, well...it is the sort of thing I might do myself," he admitted.

"You are rotten," Justin replied. "I'm glad you're on my side and not Brandon's."

Gabriel sighed. "We're all on the same side. He wants to protect you because you are necessary to the kingdom and precious to him personally."

"He might act like it." Justin wouldn't look at Gabriel.

"Come now," Gabriel said, laughing. "You couldn't even look at me when I said I loved you, and I'm your cousin. What if Brandon said something similar, and him the hardened warrior with no heart? You'd think he was possessed of a demon or something."

"Shut up," Justin muttered.

Gabriel chuckled. "You know I'm right."

"He's going to kill us both when we show up at their camp." Justin's voice shook a little.

"We can turn around and go back to the keep. I'll never breathe a word of this to anyone, if that's what you want to do." Gabriel knew better than to hope Justin would take that option, but he still held his breath until the prince snorted.

"You ought to know better. I don't turn back once I've set my hand to the plow."

"As if you've ever even seen a plow," Gabriel teased. "Well, then, how about this: we sneak into the camp and find Ranulf before doing anything? I happen to have a very fine bottle of whiskey in my pack, and if anyone could soften your knight up a bit before he finds us, it's Ran. In the meantime, you and I can settle in amongst the other Elite Corps men."

Justin was silent for so long Gabriel wondered if he'd gone to sleep in the saddle. Finally his cousin sighed. "It's as good an idea as anything I can come up with." His voice was plaintive. "I'm tired of shouting."

Gabriel snorted. "Then you might as well find a new best friend. I am quite certain Lord Shrike doesn't plan to give up shouting any time soon."

It was a pleasant night. Gabriel watched the moon climb in the sky as they rode south. It would be very late when they reached the Elite Corps' campsite. Perhaps they could slip in and spend the night before Shrike discovered them. Shrike wouldn't be happy, Justin was right about that. It *was* a risk they were taking, riding across the plains at night, just the two of them. But Gabriel had been doing it all his life, and there had only been a handful of times when he'd had any trouble, and the Bitterfruit Uprising had been out on the Free Marches, where no lord ruled.

The music of nightjars and crickets accompanied the rhythm of their horses' hooves, and once in a while they heard an owl hoot or some small prey animal shriek in fear or pain. There were few large predators that would cause them any trouble. Wolves were shy creatures that would never attack a man, especially on horseback. March lions would attack two riders, but they were rare in this area, and at this time of year, smaller game was plentiful. Gabriel found himself humming in contentment.

"You love this land, don't you?" Justin asked softly when they'd been riding about two hours.

Gabriel smiled as a star fell across the sky. "I do. Something sings in my blood when I am out on the marches like this. Perhaps it's the influence of my Shallan grandmother."

"Or the Landmagic," Justin said. "My father tells me I won't feel it truly until I am older and crowned king. But I feel a fierce, wild joy in me when I travel the kingdom, and I think it's a little hint of the Landmagic."

Gabriel shrugged. Not much was known about the Landmagic. It consecrated the true ruler of a land, and was something brought to life centuries ago when the kingdom of Teronn was established. But over the years, they had lost the crafting of it, and only loosely held the keeping of it. He didn't set much store in the Landmagic. Then again, he had been prepared to renounce his claim on Jerol, so perhaps the Landmagic didn't set much store in him.

It was nearly midnight when they reached the Elite Corps camp. Justin saw the glow of campfires first, and then Gabriel pointed out the bulk of Eagle Mountain looming against the sky beyond them.

"They'll have sentries out," Justin said. His lack of planning embarrassed him. How would they get around the sentries?

"Pull your hood up and let me do the talking. They won't understand why I'm here, but they won't question me. And it would be foolishness for me to ride out here alone, so they won't question why I have a companion with me."

Justin felt his cheeks heat at Gabriel's gentle reproach. This had been a huge mistake. But there was nothing for it but to brazen it out. He tugged his hood up to hide his face.

Gabriel exchanged pleasantries with the sentry and asked where he would find Sir Destry. The sentry, who recognized Gabriel in the light of his half-shuttered lamp, pointed them to one of the tents. With gracious thanks, Gabriel guided his horse in that direction, and Justin followed.

They dismounted when they reached the horse pickets. Gabriel removed his saddlebags and bedroll and led the way to Destry's tent. As they approached, Gabriel pursed his lips and whistled six melancholy notes. Justin glanced at him, curious, but his cousin was watching the tent.

The flap was pushed back and Sir Destry looked out, eyes wide. Justin couldn't decipher the expression on Destry's face. It seemed a strange mixture of hope, surprise, and longing. Then Destry saw Justin, and as quick as that, his face went blank, all emotions shuttered. Destry must not recognize the cloaked and hooded Justin, since his gaze went back to Gabriel.

"My Lord Gabriel," he murmured, bowing at the waist. "I was under the impression you were staying behind with the prince." His lips quirked. "Not that I object to your company, but what--"

"I *did* stay behind with the prince," Gabriel drawled. "But when His Highness demonstrated a distressing aversion to staying behind..." He spread his hands to either side in a silent declaration of innocence. "Well, I felt I had no choice but to accompany him."

Justin had no trouble discerning the consternation on Destry's face when he realized just who the cloaked and hooded figure was. Destry dropped to one knee. "Your Highness, my apologies."

"Get up, Sir Destry." Justin tried to keep the exasperation out of his voice. Destry was a superb bodyguard in all ways except one--he still hadn't realized that Justin had no patience for etiquette from people he relied upon daily to protect him body and soul. "It's far too late for such ceremony, and I'm aching to get out of the night chill."

Destry closed his mouth and stood. He nodded to Justin, then stood aside for them to enter the tent. Justin went inside, tilting his head ever so slightly to eavesdrop. His curiosity was rewarded when Gabriel's footsteps behind him paused.

"Are you insane?" Destry breathed. "Lord Shrike will burst into flames when he sees the prince."

"Indeed." Gabriel's voice was sardonic as he made no attempt to keep Justin from hearing. "But better he direct his wrath at me than at Justin. And I brought some Peregrine Whiskey to soften the news." Liquid sloshed as Gabriel shook the bottle.

Justin settled himself on Destry's cot and shucked his cloak. A small brazier kept the chill at bay. He looked at the other two men, but couldn't bring himself to meet Destry's eyes. He let his gaze drop back to the glowing coals and swallowed hard. If Destry was this disappointed in him, what would Brandon think?

This had been the stupidest decision he'd ever made.

It didn't take long enough, in Justin's opinion, for them to hear raised voices approaching the tent. One of them was Brandon, and the other... well, there was only one raised voice, Justin amended. The other person was speaking much more quietly. Probably Ranulf.

The tent flap was thrown back with enough violence the entire structure shivered. Brandon stood in the entrance, his face white with rage. Justin stood up, anticipating a shouting match. Gabriel stayed seated, his body relaxed, his hands open on the table. Despite his appearance, Justin had the idea Gabriel was watching Brandon very closely.

Ranulf stood behind Brandon, his forehead wrinkled in a worried expression. He didn't speak, but he didn't retreat, either, which sent a pulse of gratitude through Justin.

Brandon strode slowly into the tent, his gaze fixed on Justin. "I am certain," he said, his voice low, "I instructed you to remain with Lord Malnythe--" and the way he spat the name as if it tasted bad made Justin wince-- "back at the keep." His eyes were narrowed. "Perhaps I was unclear?" He stepped closer. "Perhaps I failed to impress on you the severity of my instructions."

Justin lifted his chin. He *had* disobeyed a direct order, but there was no need for Brandon to be so sarcastic. He glared back at Brandon. "I only promised to obey your orders if my life were in danger. Which it isn't."

"You ought to let me judge, seeing as I'm the one who has any experience beyond play battles and lessons."

"That isn't fair! If my father had let me go with you--"

"Just Goddess strike me dead first," Brandon growled. "You are the heir. You can't take foolish risks."

"And the people can't love a prince if they think he's a coward," Justin countered.

Brandon sucked in a breath, his nostrils flaring. "I am not arguing this with you again. The hills campaign was two years ago. Even commoners don't send stripling boys to war. No one thought anything about your staying behind."

"Twelve is old enough to squire. Twelve is old enough to--"

"Enough!" Brandon interrupted. "What made you think you could disobey my direct order?"

Justin gritted his teeth. "We felt our life was sufficiently protected by the presence of our Elite Corps." It was playing dirty to speak so formally to Brandon. The words left a bad taste in his mouth.

Brandon barked a laugh, though his gaze hardened even more. "Oh, we did, did we? And what does his royal highness know about threats to his life? Has his royal highness ever seen a horde of haonggen swarming through a village? Has his royal highness ever faced down a pack of hunting dragtuk? Has his royal highness ever lifted his blade against a man who desired his death?"

"*How could I?*" Justin shouted. "How could I, when you have me swaddled in blankets and cushions like so much fragile porcelain? How can I ever know adversity, if you won't even let me *live* my *life*!?"

From the corner of his eye he saw Gabriel make a gesture, but he didn't care what his cousin thought. He was tired of being treated like a child or an idiot. He was tired of Brandon's lack of confidence in him. And he was *extremely* tired of Brandon scolding him.

"You little fool, I am trying to ensure you have a life to live!" Brandon snarled back. Good. That cold sarcasm was gone. Justin took a step closer to him.

"I think you're so obsessed with your slavish notions of loyalty you've forgotten I'm an actual person instead of some marble statue," Justin snapped. "I'm not an ideal, Brandon. I'm a man. I'm *me*."

Brandon opened his mouth to speak, then shook his head. "You're a man? You're behaving like a child."

A chill went through Justin. Finally, Brandon said what he'd been implying for weeks. It should enrage Justin. But instead...it just felt good to have it in the open.

He cleared his throat. "Perhaps I am behaving this way because you have already made me a child in your mind." He moved closer. "Perhaps I am behaving this way because you are treating me like a child." He licked his lips. "Or...or perhaps..." Suddenly his heart was thumping in his chest. "Perhaps I am behaving this way because it seems to be the only way to get your undivided attention." His throat tightened. There. He'd spoken the truth. And somehow, it hadn't killed him. Even if he wished the ground would open up and swallow him.

Brandon was staring at him. His mouth hung open. Justin forced himself to hold Brandon's gaze. He must stand behind his words. Everything about their friendship was changing. He had to know if Brandon even cared about him anymore.

Brandon shook his head slowly. "Justin." He stepped closer and reached out, then let his hand fall before it touched Justin's shoulder. "How can you think that? I have dedicated my life to protecting you. To serving you."

Justin had to swallow twice before he could speak. "What about just being my friend?" he croaked.

Brandon simply stared at him.

Justin waved a hand. "I have dozens--hundreds--of men who protect me and serve me. I have scores of soldiers and servants at my beck and call. I have lackeys and vassals who are eager for my good opinion." He laughed sadly. "None of that matters, Bran. Not if I don't have someone who listens to me. Someone who treats me as if I'm Justin, not the prince or his royal highness or the heir to the throne."

Brandon's jaw worked. "I...I didn't..."

"You've always been that for me, Bran. My best friend. I know you're older, and I know you have a life, you have-- duties and other friends and--" He shrugged. "And lands I gave you myself, for the love of the Saints, that you should probably visit more than once every year or two. But..." He lifted a hand, palm up. "But I want my best friend back."

Brandon bowed his head. His breathing had gone ragged. Gabriel slipped out of his chair and took Ranulf's elbow. They disappeared outside.

Brandon sighed deeply and sat in a chair. "You were still a damn fool for riding out here with just your cousin for company," he growled.

Justin could have laughed. "I know. I'm lucky he knew what I was going to do, or I would have ridden out here alone."

"He should have locked you in your room. Vallu's teeth! What if you'd come across a band of hostile Horse Clan? There are march lions and wolves out this way, for that matter. And there could be haonggen. Or dragtuk even."

"I hardly think the Dark King's hounds could be hunting this far south without our having heard something about it," Justin said dryly. Saints, he should have been honest with Brandon weeks ago.

Brandon scowled at him. "Don't think I'm letting you *or* your cousin off the hook for this ridiculous stunt. *You* may be an impetuous, big-hearted, damnfool fourteen-year-old, but Malnythe is supposed to have a head on his shoulders. If he can't bring himself to think about your safety before his own, perhaps he isn't fit for the Elite Corps after all."

Justin rolled his eyes. "You are obsessed. No one but you cares about that, and I'm tired of hearing it. Come on, Bran. I know for a fact Gabriel sent Ranulf to your tent with a bottle of Grivyth whiskey. You may not like the fact I'm here, but you'll have to live with it. I command you to complete the exercise you came here to run. And in the meantime, I ask you--" He gave Brandon a lopsided grin. "--to share your whiskey with me."

"You shouldn't be drinking anything stronger than ale," Brandon muttered, but he was already turning toward the exit. "You'll sleep in my tent, and your idiot cousin can stand guard while I get my beauty rest. Come on, Prince Bratling. Let's go taste that whiskey."

CHAPTER FIVE

And here I ended up taking part in the Elite Corps exercise after all, thought Gabriel as he watched the losing team straggle back into camp. Brandon had even allowed Justin to participate. Gabriel knew there would still be a price to pay for his own disrespect for Brandon's wishes, but at least the Prince's Knight had softened towards Justin.

Gabriel sighed and led his horse to the picket. Winners and losers alike were brushing their horses, their teasing punctuated by laughter. Gabriel found a spot among them, near enough to observe Ranulf without being noticed.

Ranulf was well-liked, Gabriel could see. He bantered with two of the losers; one of them, a short, dark-complected man, was promising retaliation in their next exercise. They were close, these men, and Gabriel had seen how efficiently they fought together. Perhaps he had been wrong to avoid joining them. He chewed his lip, running his brush down the wet line where the saddle girth had been. The camaraderie was tempting.

"Don't worry," said a low voice. "There's no place for you here."

Gabriel looked up to find Brandon watching him. His gaze was hard. Gabriel had seen those blue eyes soften when Brandon looked at Justin, but there was no give in them for Gabriel.

"After all the trouble you've taken to secure me for the Elite Corps, you are now withdrawing the offer?" Gabriel smirked at Brandon and found the act enjoyable. "Lord Shrike, I had no idea you were such a changeable man."

Brandon took a half step closer, his hands clenching into fists. "That's the wolf calling the lion a killer," he hissed. "You are in no position to mock me, Malnythe, after the way you endangered Justin and encouraged him to ignore the advice of more experienced men."

It surprised Gabriel how much Brandon's opprobrium stung. Brandon had never had much use for him; why did it matter if he now disliked Gabriel outright? Gabriel shrugged. "You and I have very different values, Lord Shrike, but I feel we can still part on friendly terms. After all, we have my cousin in common, and we both wish to see him safe and happy."

"Do we?" Brandon sneered. "You are rather cavalier with the things you profess to love, Malnythe. I shall have to warn Destry to take care."

Gabriel sucked in a breath, ready to snap at him, and only just managed to catch himself. But rising to Brandon's bait would only let him know his words had opened a wound. Gabriel lifted his chin and tossed his hair out of his face. "I suppose you will think whatever you wish. At least if you have found me wanting, I shall feel no further obligation to serve in the Elite Corps." He gave Brandon a tiny smile and turned his attention back to his horse.

He could feel the man still fuming behind him, but Gabriel refused to give him any further satisfaction. If Shrike was determined to hate him...well, let him. Justin knew better.

Everyone gathered some time later for Brandon to go over the action and analyze what had been done well and what ill. Gabriel listened idly, but he took generous sips from his flask of mead. He was more interested in watching Justin. His cousin had been on the winning side with Ranulf and Gabriel, and was flush with the victory. He almost looked his age, instead of the solemn young man he so often appeared to be.

Gabriel was struck with a pang of loneliness for Chid and Arthi. They had been much younger than he, but they had loved him and looked up to him, and he had grumbled about how they got into his papers and hid his books. He took a long drink of his mead and caught Shrike watching him. A spark of animosity flashed between them, and Gabriel smiled faintly. It was an accomplishment, he supposed, to be a burr under the saddle of so important a man as the Prince's Knight. It gave him a lot to live up to.

So when the briefing was finished, Gabriel went back to his tent and unpacked the bags he'd brought with him. Six jars of Sweetgrass Mead that someone back home was bound to miss, and he'd sent two casks of it with Ranulf in the supply wagon. Humming to himself, Gabriel went to break open the casks and declare a celebration.

The announcement was greeted with cheers from the soldiers and a silent, smoldering glower from Shrike. Perfect. Gabriel collared Justin and found them a place to sit out of the way of the rough-housing and dancing that began after the first cask was emptied. The soldiers passed around a headscarf and apron, taking turns at playing the lady and attempting some of the rowdier folk dances. When he saw Ranulf in that getup, Justin began giggling so hard he nearly fell out of his chair.

When Ranulf took off the scarf and apron and offered them to Brandon, Justin burped, turned green, and leaned over to vomit. Despite his amusement at the sight of the dour Shrike prancing and kicking, Gabriel jumped up to steady Justin.

"There, just a bit too much, eh?" he murmured, and felt bad when Justin moaned and leaned against his chest. It was so easy to forget how young Justin was, in some ways, at least. Gabriel got one of the other men to follow with a pitcher of cold water while Gabriel carried his cousin to bed. When Justin finally fell asleep, Gabriel headed back to the festivities, but his heart was no longer in it.

The next morning, Gabriel had gone from being the most popular man in camp to the least. Everyone walked softly, eyes squinted against the light. Justin took two bites of his breakfast and ran for the privy trench to throw up again.

All the same, they managed to break camp and get moving by mid-morning. They were out of the shadow of Eagle Mountain when they stopped for lunch, by which time some of the men had forgiven Gabriel. Justin was able to keep down his lunch, and he actually thanked Gabriel for letting him drink as much as he wanted.

"I don't expect I shall ever want to drink that much again," he assured Gabriel, expression solemn.

Remembering how often he'd made himself just that same promise, only to break it the next time he was caught up in revelry, Gabriel refrained from laughing and only ruffled Justin's hair.

They were an hour from Jerol Keep when the two forward scouts came galloping back to the main company, leaving a wake of dust behind them.

"Bitterfruit raiders!" one of them gasped. "At least two score of them!"

Brandon swore. "Wheel right. We'll go around--"

"No use, sir," interrupted the other scout. "They've seen us. We'll have to fight."

"Vallu's teeth!" Brandon snarled. He swung around, his gaze finding Gabriel. "This is your fault, Malnythe. If anything happens to Justin, I'll have your head."

His voice carried, ensuring that not only did Ranulf and the rest of the Elite Corps hear, but Justin did as well.

"Justin is right here, Brandon," the prince said, straightening in his saddle. "And nothing will happen to him, because he is a trained warrior himself."

"With no battle experience and shaky from drink!" Brandon snapped. "First group, cluster around the prince. Sell your lives dear if the savages reach you! Second and third groups, take the left and right flanks. Make sure none of them get around behind us. Groups four through six, with me. We'll line up on the crest of that rise up ahead."

Justin guided his horse closer to his cousin, who had thankfully stayed by him. For all his brave words, he suspected his mouth was dry and his hands shaking from more than the hangover. He had never fought in a real battle before. Even Gabriel, with his gentle heart, had fought against the Bitterfruit when they rose up against the king and burned a village.

"You'll be fine," Gabriel murmured. He had guided his horse so close their knees were touching. "The only Bitterfruit left are cowards; they hit fast and run away to hide. One charge and they'll probably turn tail."

Justin managed a sickly smile. "I know." He'd studied the uprising from a distance, even if his father hadn't allowed him to fight. Uncle Frewyn had called on his Horse Clan allies and soldiers from Port Kama, and together they had put down the rebellion. The rebellious clan had been splintered. Most of those surviving had slunk off to the Tsareng Foothills in the south. A raid this far north was unusual, though not unheard of.

The circle of warriors around them tightened. Gabriel snapped, "We need enough room to swing a sword, unless one of you is interested in losing a hand!" The crush lessened after that.

Hooves crashed against the ground with such force he glanced up to be certain it wasn't thunder. Justin heard a great crash that must be the two sides meeting. Men yelled in two languages, horses neighed, and swords clashed. Brandon's voice rose above the chaos, shouting orders. Justin strained to see past his human shield. He felt like his heart had jumped into his throat and was pounding there.

A dozen of the rebels broke through and came up in front of Justin's group. They wailed in their strange tongue, some wielding spears and others wielding swords.

Justin, sword drawn, braced himself, but Gabriel slipped between Justin and the nearest rebel. His sword flashed twice and the rebel sprawled on the ground. Two more attacked Gabriel, one distracting him while the other hit his knee with a club. Gabriel dispatched the first, but yelled at the pain and faltered. Sir Riush chopped his sword down at the second. Then the other Elite Corps warriors closed around Justin and Gabriel. The battle was over before Justin could do anything but watch.

"I could have fought!" Justin cried, glaring. Gabriel's face was sweaty and strained.

"I know you could have," Gabriel bit out. "But I draw the line at allowing you to fight when you have a perfectly good guard with you."

Justin scowled. "You're hurt."

"The bastard clubbed my leg. I'll have a nasty bruise, but that's all."

Justin took a long breath, held it, then let it go. His heart was still racing in his chest, and he was unaccountably angry, but Gabriel didn't deserve his temper. "I'm glad it isn't serious."

"So am I." Gabriel nudged his horse closer. "Jus, this was bad. If we'd run into this band on our way out, just you and I, instead of--"

"Hush," Justin ordered. He forced a smile. "I'm certain I shall hear enough of it from Brandon. I would hate to be lectured twice."

Gabriel's laugh was choked, but it reassured Justin, at least for as long as it took for Brandon to arrive at a gallop.

"Where's the Prince?" Brandon's call was urgent.

Justin urged his horse past Gabriel's. "Here."

Brandon grabbed him by the elbow as soon as he was within reach. He turned in the saddle to peer into Justin's face. "You're unhurt?"

Justin swallowed. He'd never seen such fear in Brandon's gaze. "I--" he croaked, and coughed. "I'm unhurt."

Brandon squeezed Justin's arm hard and tipped his head back, staring into the hot blue sky. After a moment he sighed. "Healer? We've wounded." Justin looked past Brandon to the rest of the group. One of the warriors led a limping horse, and another man was slumped against his horse's neck.

"Yes, sir." One of Justin's guards slung his shield over his back and galloped to meet the approaching group. Only then did Justin realize the man had no blade; Healers were sworn against harming others, but apparently an Elite Corps Healer was at least allowed to defend himself. Brandon released Justin's arm and followed the Healer.

Gabriel sucked in an audible breath. Justin glanced at him and saw his cousin staring, white-faced, after them. When Justin looked again, he realized the warrior lying along his horse's neck was Ranulf Destry. Destry's shoulder looked wrong--lumpy and misshapen--and blood stained the side of his breeches as well.

Gabriel galloped after them. After one look at Brandon's face, Justin sent a silent plea to the Merciful God and urged his horse up between Gabriel and Brandon. Brandon's face was white, his sword arm rigid, and Justin didn't trust him not to damage Gabriel. Which wasn't fair, since Gabriel looked distraught enough over Ranulf's injury. It must be that blasted sword saying something vile in Brandon's head.

"I hope you're happy with yourself," Brandon was saying as Justin arrived. "If you hadn't--"

"Would have--run into them--" Ranulf panted. Good, he was conscious, at least. "--in any event--"

"Shh." Gabriel steadied Ranulf against him, then nodded to the Healer. The Healer had taken off one of his boots, which struck Justin as odd. A moment later, the man stuck his foot in Ranulf's armpit and tugged on his arm.

Ranulf cried out and Justin heard, even above his voice, an audible crack. Ranulf slumped against Gabriel's chest, breathing hard. Justin's stomach did a tumble, but he swallowed hard and fought the nausea.

"I'll get some easetea in you to cut the pain," the Healer said. "It isn't fresh, so it won't be as effective, and it's cold, so you'll want to toss your fritters. But it'll be worth it."

Ranulf nodded without speaking and took the flask with his good hand. He gulped it down and grimaced.

Gabriel's face was stricken as he looked down at Ranulf. His lower lip was between his teeth, worrying at it. Ranulf must have felt his tension, because he looked up at Gabriel.

"Don't, Gabriel," he murmured. "You didn't put them out here."

"That doesn't make it any better," Gabriel whispered.

"I've been hurt worse than this." Humor flickered across Ranulf's face. "T'was the Bitterfruit last time as well, as I recall." His voice was loosening. "I'll heal, as I did before."

Gabriel bowed his head. "It's never been my fault before," he choked. "Damn it!"

"Hush." Ranulf's eyes were closing. Justin wondered if the easetea was taking effect, or if Ranulf was trying to end the argument. He glanced at Gabriel and flinched from the naked emotion on his cousin's face. It wasn't Gabriel's fault, it was Justin's. This was what it meant to be heir to a crown--to be responsible for those who served you, and feel hurts taken in your name as keenly as your own. He swallowed, his mouth suddenly dry. He had been selfish, and he must make amends.

They carried Ranulf on a litter between two pack horses and let the warrior with the wounded horse ride Ranulf's horse. It made for slow going, but they arrived back at the manor house before dark. There the Healer did a second Healing of Ranulf's leg and said he would be hale by the end of the week. Justin saw Brandon relax, but the next moment he tensed again and rounded on Gabriel, who had been waiting, head bowed, for the Healer's pronouncement.

"Your foolishness nearly got Ranulf killed," he spat. "We had a horse injured, you yourself were injured, and Justin was in danger. All because you thought it would be fun to bring the prince out against my express wishes and get everyone drunk. You're a disgrace. You've no concept of responsibility or duty. You've no sense of honor. You aren't fit to be a member of the Elite Corps. You're not even fit to be a member of the nobility."

"Brandon!" Justin made his voice sharp. "That is enough."

Brandon turned on him. "Is it? Do you understand the dangers we faced today? Your loving cousin--"

"I apologize," Justin said, as calmly as he could. The interruption stopped Brandon's tirade. "I was foolish to go against your wishes, Bran. I know that. While I enjoyed the exercise and learned a great deal, I also realize I should have leaned on your experience as a warrior. For my indiscretions, I humbly apologize. If things had gone badly, my father might have punished you, and I would hate for us to be separated. I will learn to consider the potential costs of my actions."

Brandon opened his mouth. After several heartbeats, he cleared his throat and looked away. "Well. You needn't go quite that far. I don't feel you were to blame. You are young, and while you are wise and responsible for your age, you haven't the experience we have. Lord Malnythe, however--"

"Gabriel did his best to curb my temper and impulsiveness," Justin broke in. "He is, however, astute enough to know when he has not been successful, and clever enough to adjust his strategy accordingly. When I would not be dissuaded from riding out to the Elite Corps camp, he determined to ride with me. I daresay his behavior protected me rather than endangering me."

Brandon folded his arms across his chest, raising one eyebrow. "And the Sweetgrass Mead?"

It was Justin's turn to look away. "I confess, I am uncertain why anyone would wish to overindulge in strong drink. Perhaps Gabriel was over-generous with his libations, but I would argue your warriors should know their own limits and keep to them." He glanced up at Brandon from beneath his fringe. When he saw Brandon's lips twitch, he permitted himself a tiny smile. "I have certainly learned mine."

"You are a rascal," Brandon told him. His gaze hardened as he turned it on Gabriel. "I don't agree with your cousin, but as he insists on taking up for you, I can see I am powerless to demand satisfaction of you. However, I stand by my statement you are not fit to be a member of the Elite Corps."

Justin thought Gabriel must have been holding his breath, judging by his little sigh. Gabriel bowed. "I must submit to your judgment in this case, Lord Shrike."

"Yes, you must." Brandon's voice wasn't friendly, but at least the outright hostility had gone out of it. Justin would have to settle for that.

CHAPTER SIX

Ranulf perched on the edge of his seat, his posture stiff. The gash in his leg was healed, and his shoulder only bothered him when he reached too far, but Gabriel still felt bad. He sighed and leaned forward, resting his elbows on his knees.

"Ran, I'm so terribly sorry," he said. "I'm a fool. I hope you won't be punished for my mistakes." He sensed some of the tension leaving his friend. "Lord Shrike has determined I do not belong in the Elite Corps. I could have told him that myself, but I confess, I didn't mean to go about it quite like this. But I am certain he sees your worth. You are most welcome to stay and serve here at Jerol. You know it would please me. But I would also be pleased if you choose to return to Laurenstat as a member of the Elite Corps. Though I have no right to be, I am proud of you for what you have done there."

"Gabriel." Ranulf shook his head, holding Gabriel's gaze. "The only reason I could stand to be parted from you is to do this service to the king." His voice sounded thick. "All I do, I do in your name. You have already served King Godfric and Prince Justin well, but I aspire to yet serve them better for your honor." He swallowed. "Otherwise I would happily stay here and help you however was in my power. But..."

Gabriel's eyes started stinging at those words. He could live without Shrike's good opinion, as long as Justin and Ranulf still believed in him. "I understand," he whispered. "And you have my blessing."

Ranulf gripped Gabriel's hand. For several heartbeats neither of them spoke, then Gabriel cleared his throat and sat back. "Well. We have spicecake and whiskey and a good fire. If we're to part again tomorrow, we might as well make the most of tonight."

"Gabriel?" Jon stopped just inside the door. "The prince and his company are nearly ready to depart. I've had the chatelaine prepare the parting cup."

Gabriel drew in a long breath and held it. This visit had set things in motion, and he had a feeling he would be feeling the ramifications for years to come. He nodded. "Have there been any problems?"

Jon grinned. "Well, the chatelaine has been asking questions about some missing casks of Sweetgrass Mead. I believe Sergeant Savona implied the Elite Corps might have requisitioned them. I believe she is preparing a belated bill of sale."

Gabriel laughed. "Take that, Brandon Shrike."

"Ahem. Just so." Jon studied his fingernails for a moment. "Have you, ah, decided what you will do with yourself after the prince and Ranulf are gone?"

"Am I that transparent?" Gabriel stifled the rush of depression that thought inspired. He didn't want to watch his cousin leave and be left to brood over his mistakes. Jon knew him too well.

Jon shrugged. "Perhaps it would be good to travel a bit. We could head north for a visit to the highlands, perhaps come home through the capital in the autumn."

That was a very good idea. "Thank the Merciful God for you, Jon. I would be lost without you."

Smiling, Jon bowed and gestured for Gabriel to lead the way out of the room. "I shall take every opportunity to remind you, my lord."

ABOUT THE AUTHOR

Stephanie A. Cain writes epic and urban fantasy for fun, and a history blog for work. She lives in Indiana. She enjoys hiking, reading, birdwatching, and general geekery. She has three cats, which she is well aware puts her firmly in crazy cat lady territory, and way more dice and painted miniatures than she needs.

A QUICK NOTE

Thanks for reading my novella. If you enjoyed this, would you please take a moment to leave a review of my book at Amazon, Barnes & Noble, or Goodreads? Writing just two or three honest sentences is one of the best things you can do to support an indie author like me.

Thanks!

Stephanie

CONNECT WITH ME ONLINE:

Website: stephaniecainonline.com
Facebook: facebook.com/stephaniecainfiction
Twitter: twitter.com/stephanie_cain
Pinterest: pinterest.com/writersteph/